A HUMAN CYBORG

YASHVI JALAN

"Life is an incessant river with small islands all around. In order to cross these islands one needs some slefless and loyal boatsmen. " - Yashvi Jalan

Contents

Foreword

Sometimes wanting a revenge can cause you more pain than satisfaction.

Preface

A book about how even machines can want justice, fall in love and be angry.

Prologue

My name is James Pattinson. I am 16 years old and busy completing high school. So here's a peek into the incidents that changed my life forever.

First Impression

Her hair was mercury red and it tumbled over her shoulders. Her eyebrows were slender and her eyes were torrent black. She had a dainty nose and saccharine sweet lips. Her teeth were halo-white. She had a sculptured figure and tapered waist with carmine red fingernails. She was draped in an elegant dress with high heels. Mrs. Jonas, our principal, walked beside the heavenly stranger and introduced her as our new English teacher, Ms. Emma Adison. She formally greeted us and my gaze locked with hers and suddenly I felt she X- Rayed me from top to bottom and her blinking was very minimal. I looked away after being subjected to this peculiar gaze. Not intending to know what had just happened, I considered it to be a hallucination.

CHAPTER TWO

Uncanny Observations

During the lunch break, while absentmindedly strolling in the garden Ms. Adison nonchalantly pricked her delicate fingers with the thorns of the cactus. To my bewilderment, my eyes couldn't spot even a drop of blood. I interpreted it to be my misconception. During the fifth period, Ms. Adison muttered her prolonged speech, uninterrupted, not even pausing to catch a breath and her handwriting was similar to that of my computer's font- Comic Sans MS. As the bell rang, she went forward to take the attendance and after a teeny-weeny glance of the register, she had memorised the names of my classmates successfully and called them out confidently. I now had a sneaking suspicion that our new teacher was different from the others.

CHAPTER THREE

The Truth

As soon as I returned home, I went through those uncanny observations again and recalled reading about something related to it. Before I could uncover the truth, my phone rang and it was my best friend, Bob. He as usual made fun of the new teacher and frankly told that he found Ms. Emma Adison to be just like a machine because of her weird mannerisms. Eureka! I left the phone unattended and realised that Ms. Edison was nothing but a cyborg. The following day, I confronted her and now she could not refrain but admit the truth.

CHAPTER FOUR

Peek into the Past

She then on her own accord gave an explanation, 'A few decades ago, I was just a jovial human girl who lived with her parents in a bungalow near the countryside. 12th April 1978, was probably the last day of my contentment. My father had received a call from some unknown number and he was immediately panic- stricken. He loaded our daily requirements into the car and ordered us to briskly get in. I was perplexed but did not question him. Before we could reach our undisclosed location, our car was bombarded. Next, I remember waking in a cell. However, the environment I was subjected to was unfamiliar

Transformation

After a few ticks of the clock, two masked people marched in and before I could say something, they injected some sort of serum into me. I fell motionless on the ground and could feel fire burning within me as every moment passed. My memories as a human were casted like a film in front of me. My body was stiffening like steel and I could feel a reel of data and pictures swirling in my mind. My fingers turned out to be more cylindrical than ever and I felt way more energetic. My eyes were scanning the things around and a virtual keypad appeared in front of my eyes.'

CHAPTER SIX

The Manual-Computerized Factory

'Though my supernatural eyes I saw through the doors, my father tied to a chair weeping continuously. A towering lady stood beside him and kept criticising him for betraying her trust. He then said "You have already killed my wife, now do you plan to kill the only ray of hope in my life, my daughter?" Annoyed, she burst out, "I did not murder your wife she could not survive the robotic transformation but I must say your daughter is doing great." I did not know whether I should have mourned over the fact that my mom had left me, or be astounded by the fact that I was a robot, or save my father. Amidst the plethora of thoughts, the wicked lady went on "You were the one Adison who came up with the idea of making robots out of humans and using them to change Earth and remove the humans from here so that we could be the leaders and this foolish world that could never respect our abilities realises its status. They never acknowledged our ideas. Then how could you betray us.... you traitor!!?" I could not believe that my father was the villain all this time. I could not stand to hear the truth and broke out of the place.', 'Since that day I haven't grown either. I have remained 18.' She added, trying to be hilarious.

CHAPTER SEVEN

Guilt

I could see guilt in Emma's eyes, she tried to cry but tears failed to come out of her eyes. I hugged her and we went on to complete the voyage which could either kill us or be the end of those monsters. The journey to the laboratory was a tiring one but we somehow managed to sneak and crossed paths with none other than Mr. Edison. He was delighted to see his daughter but Emma acted indifferently. She no longer felt connected to him and simply confronted him, 'You were never worthy to be my father. So, you better stay away from me I hate you and I don't want to see your face for the rest of my life.' Mr. Edison said, 'I know...I am guilty and I am really sorry but I had no other choice. They wanted to use you as the trial robot because you had o- blood group that was the only condition required for the serum to work. I could not sacrifice you so I ran away but then.... you know what happened next. But give me a chance to prove my love for you and try seek forgiveness for this unforgiveable act of mine. The day you ran, I had planned to take revenge for the injustice towards you and today I am finally executing what I had planned. I have installed bombs everywhere possible and they may burst any minute before that I will go and get the serum so that nobody may misuse it.'

CHAPTER EIGHT

The End

Meanwhile, Emma had planned to forgive her father but before Mr. Adison could come out with the serum the bomb went active and flames burst out from all corners of the factory. Emma was inconsolable and all I could do was promise to take care of her as long as I am alive.